Fancy Feet

by Abby Jackson

Consultant: Mindy Craft, Apparel Designer
WSI Sports

Yellow
Umbrella
Books
for early readers

Yellow Umbrella Books are published by Red Brick Learning
7825 Telegraph Road, Bloomington, Minnesota 55438
http://www.redbricklearning.com

Editorial Director: Mary Lindeen
Senior Editor: Hollie J. Endres
Senior Designer: Gene Bentdahl
Photo Researcher: Signature Design
Developer: Raindrop Publishing
Consultant: Mindy Craft, Apparel Designer, WSI Sports
Conversion Assistants: Jenny Marks, Laura Manthe

Library of Congress Cataloging-in-Publication Data
Jackson, Abby
  Fancy Feet / by Abby Jackson
     p. cm.
  Includes index.
  ISBN 0-7368-5847-4 (hardcover)
  ISBN 0-7368-5277-8 (softcover)
  1. Shoes—Juvenile literature. I. Title. II. Series.
  GT2130.J33 2005
  391.4'13—dc22
                                            2005015712

Photo Credits:
Cover: Corbis; Title Page: Kathy Willens/AP/Wide World Photos; Page 2: Jupiter Images; Page 3: Gianni Dagli Orti/Corbis; Page 4: Hulton Archive/Getty Images, Inc.; Page 5: Alinari/Art Resource, NY; Page 6: Corbis Sygma; Page 7: Gilbert Patrick/Corbis Sygma; Page 8: Alinari/Art Resource, NY; Page 9: Gilbert Patrick/Corbis Sygma; Page 10: Corbis; Page 11: AP/Wide World Photos; Page 12: Corel; Pages 13 and 14: Jupiter Images

1 2 3 4 5 6 11 10 09 08 07 06

Table of Contents

On Your Toes

Your feet help you dance or walk down the street. They help you run and jump and skate. Your feet do a great job of getting you from place to place. How do you **protect** them? You wear shoes.

Early shoes were made from leaves, vines, or animal skins. People living in different places made different kinds of shoes. Those who walked on the hot desert sand made sandals. People who walked in the snow made warm, furry boots.

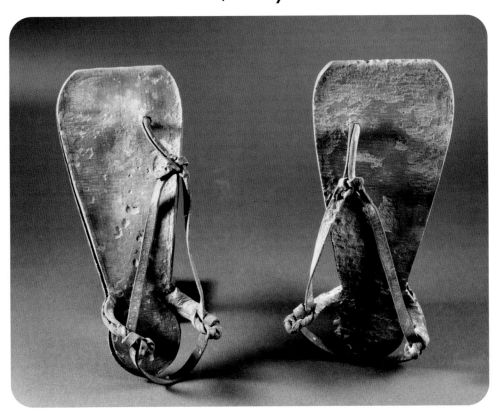

Changing Shoes

Over time people were able to make shoes in different shapes. Look at these shoes with long, pointed toes! This type of shoe was worn during the Middle Ages. The richest, most powerful people wore the shoes with the longest toes.

Long ago, the peasants in Europe wore wooden shoes. Each shoe was carved by hand. These shoes were called **sabots**. Some people still wear this type of shoe today.

About 500 years ago, women began to
wear tall shoes. These were not the
same as the high heels you see today.
A whole platform lifted a woman up.
Sometimes her feet would be as high as
18 inches (45.7 cm) off the ground!

In George Washington's day, buckles and bows **decorated** both men's and women's shoes. Children's shoes also came in bold colors, such as these bright red ones.

Making Shoes

For a long time people didn't have different shoes for the right and left feet. Both shoes were the same. About 200 years ago people began making right and left shoes. At first, people thought they looked silly. They called them "crooked shoes."

Long ago, people didn't go to a shoe store to buy a new pair of shoes. They would visit a **shoemaker**. The shoemaker made shoes one at a time. Shoemakers used a wooden tool to measure each shoe. This tool was called a **last**.

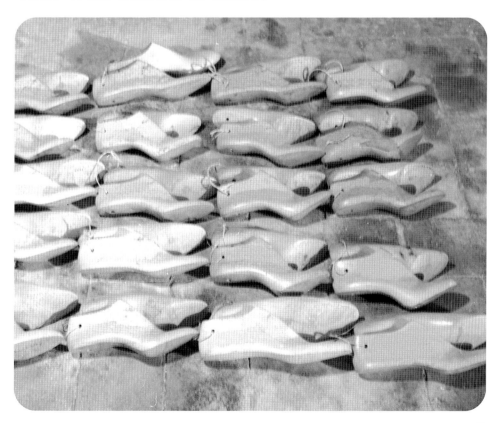

What invention helped to make a greater number of shoes more easily? It was the sewing machine! Once the sewing machine was invented, people could stitch and sew shoes quickly. People began to own more than just one pair of shoes.

How are shoes made today? They are made in **factories**. When the shoes are finished they are shipped to shoe stores around the world. Today, it is easy to walk into a store and pick out your new shoes.

Different Kinds of Shoes

People wear many different kinds of shoes. Special shoes help people walk on ice, climb mountains, and dive deep into the ocean. This astronaut wears boots that were made to help him walk on the moon.

Scientists are always looking for new and better **materials** for making shoes. Runners wear shoes that help them run faster. Shoes also help protect a runner's feet from injury.

Even though shoes have changed over the years, one thing is still the same. Whether they are fancy or plain, big or small, shoes protect our feet!

Glossary

decorate—to add extra things to something to make it look nice

factories—large buildings where people make products for people

last—a wooden block shaped like a foot that was used to make shoes

materials—what things are made of, such as plastic, cotton, or paper

protect—to keep safe

sabots—carved, wooden, clog-like shoes

shoemaker—a person who make shoes

Index

Word Count: 474
Early-Intervention Level: M